At the Grand Canyon the Wild Turkey is found living in the Kaibab forest on the north side or the North Rim. The Wild Turkey is an American bird of the pheasant family. It is a beautiful multi-colored bird of trim form and long, slim legs. It usually weighs 12 to 14 pounds. The Wild Turkey's natural habitat is the forest, but it will enter clearings to run and feed. Its diet consists of acorns, seeds, berries, and insects. During mating season the male (gobbler) calls the females (hens) to him. A simple nest on the ground is common.

I AM AN ARO PUBLISHING 60 WORD BOOK
MY 60 WORDS ARE:

a	he (he's)	the
any	I	them
are	in	there
at	is	those
beautiful	let	thought
because	look	through
better	made	to
canyon	most	too
chasing	my	trails
ever	name	turkey
eyes	not	two
face	on	us
fast	run (running)	want
fun	said	was
gleam	seem	we
gobble	seen	were
golden	sees	where
grand	shade	wild
grass	something	with
has (had)	Sue	you

GRAND CANYON CRITTERS

WILD TURKEY RUN

BY BOB REESE

 ARO PUBLISHING

W

On wild turkey grass
where there isn't any shade,

**A wild turkey runs
on trails that he's made.**

Through the golden grass
wild turkey sees a gleam.

The most beautiful turkey face
he's ever seen.

"Gobble," said wild turkey,

"I want to run with you."

"Gobble," said the turkey,
"My name is Turkey Sue."

"Let's run to Grand Canyon.

Let's run in the sun."

"Let's run to Grand Canyon,

because, Grand Canyon is fun."

"The turkeys are running fast.

Look at those two.

Something is chasing them.

We had better run too!"

"We thought something was chasing

you two in the sun."

"We were running to Grand Canyon

because Grand Canyon is fun."